IRONBOUND

SETH
EDGARDE

BLACKBIRD BOOKS
NEW YORK • LOS ANGELES

Cataloging-in-Publication Data

Edgarde, Seth.
Ironbound / Seth Edgarde.
p. cm.
1. Newark (N.J.)—Fiction. 2. Crime—Fiction.
3. Salvage—Fiction. I. Title.
PS3605.D4564 I76 2021 813'.6—dc23 2021930497

Blackbird Books
www.bbirdbooks.com
email us at editor@bbirdbooks.com

ISBN 978-1-61053-048-4

First Edition

10 9 8 7 6 5 4 3 2 1

IRONBOUND

I

I was born in that section of the city down neck of the Passaic River, with railroad tracks penning it in on all sides, called the Ironbound. My father ran a tug boat out of Port Newark, and every Saturday, he'd take me out on the harbor, over Newark Bay, through the Kill Van Kull, to Upper New York Bay, escorting the big freighters back out through the Narrows. Sometimes, he'd let me steer, but mostly I'd just watch, sitting and eating broken cookies, hot from the Burry Factory on Frelinghuysen Avenue, and Taylor Ham sandwiches on round rolls that my mother had made for me. She died when I was six, and, two years later, my father moved us across the Hudson to Manhattan.

He was an old Coast Guard man, and he knew how to sail. He taught me about the tides and currents, how to buck them and ride them in. Sometimes when we were out on the water after my mother had died, we'd stop for lunch, pulling in at the Atlas Yacht

Club on Constable Hook in Bayonne and heading over to Nick's Luncheonette.

He told me that the Dutch called that spit of land sticking into the harbor, between Newark and New York Bays, the Kull—the neck. When *his* grandmother was a girl, it was a weekend escape from the City, for the rich and famous, before the refinery came. But the boat club was still there, a remnant, tucked into the side of the Hook, surrounded by the refinery, in a small inlet of the Kill Van Kull, the tidal strait separating Staten Island from New Jersey, connecting the two bays.

My father died a dozen years later, broken by the waterfront mob. I went to his funeral and haven't been back to Newark since.

But I'm thinking about it now. That's where I met Jake and his sister Ellen. They were born there too and lived down the block. He was my best friend, and she was the pesky little sister who grew up to be a great beauty. They were dark, like the Portuguese, but their family was from Iran. They'd escaped after the Islamic Revolution in 1979, several years before Jake was born. His mother was a big fan of American movies and named him after the Jack Nicholson character in Chinatown. Ellen came two years later, and we'd let her tag along on our adventures or when we went out to play.

By the time I went off to college on a sailing scholarship at the Webb Institute out on the Island, I hadn't seen him in almost ten years. But there he was, a fellow freshman, also on scholarship. We were inseparable after that. It was like no time at all had passed. But it had. When I saw Ellen, I could hardly believe my eyes. She was perfect in every way. I couldn't take my eyes off of her. The thought of touching her made me crazy. When we made eye contact, it seemed like there was no one else in the world.

But there was. Jake. He had always been protective of his little sister, but as we went through college, he became even more so. I kept my thoughts to myself, and so did she.

My father died my junior year and left me a little money and a small boat docked in Brooklyn. Jake's folks had died several years before that and left him and his sister their house in Newark and a small nest egg. They sold the house to some distant relatives, and when we combined it all, it was enough to start a marine salvage business, based out of Vinegar Hill, just off the Brooklyn Navy Yard. One of our teachers at Webb helped get us started. We refitted my dad's old boat and used some of our professor's contacts to build the business.

Before long, we were on our way. We retrieved a sunken yacht off the south shore of Long Island and a shipment of lead bars that had gone overboard in a storm out on the Sound. Then there were the broken and damaged boats that we fixed and refloated inside and outside of the harbor. And there was work for the police, retrieving weapons and evidence that was too difficult or costly for them to get themselves. And there were the people who couldn't go to the police: a man who wanted an item as small as a pen drive containing videos of his wife's infidelities, thrown off a boat into the East River; a safety deposit box with $100,000 in cash, from who-knows-where, dumped in the bay, no doubt, to avoid the authorities.

The work was hard, but I loved it. Jake and I were out on the boat all day, and Ellen stayed back at the office, taking care of the books and the billing. When we'd pull back into the pier, it would be just the three of us.

Then, one day, Jake was out with a cold, and I had to pull an engine from a wrecked boat in dry dock. I came back filthy, covered in grease, and I went straight into the shower that we had in the back of the office. Ellen brought me a fresh towel and a change of clothes, and we talked through the door. It was hard to hear so I cracked it a bit, and she saw me.

I wanted her so badly I thought I would burst. I dressed quickly, before I had a chance to think about it. And then she came in, and I saw the look in her eyes. She hugged me, and I held her. Our cheeks touched and she whispered in my ear in Persian, telling me that she loved me.

I never felt so good in my life. I whispered the same words back. I had learned a fair bit of Persian, especially after my mother died, and my father started to drink. It seemed like I spent just about every night at their house down the block, listening to their parents and their grandmother talk around the kitchen table. When I would stay over, we'd end up doing the same, talking by flashlight under a blanket-tent, planning our next adventure.

Her mother, Yasmin, would read Rumi's poetry to us in the original Persian, and later, when we were alone, Ellen would recite her favorite, *The Guesthouse,* from memory. "This is *your* guesthouse," she would tell me, and it made me feel welcome and cared about, and I would look into her eyes and silently echo the line from Hafiz: *I have seen you heal a hundred deep wounds with one glance from your spectacular eyes.*

Persian became for us a secret language, secret from the other kids who knew Portuguese or Spanish. But we weren't kids anymore, and it wasn't going to work with Jake; and Jake would go crazy if he found out. So we decided not to do anything about our long-simmering feelings for one another. That lasted for all of two days.

I had bought her a volume of Rumi's poetry and brought it to her at her apartment in Brooklyn that Saturday afternoon. As she held it and looked up at me, her eyes melted my heart. She touched my hand, and I kissed her, right there in the hallway, outside her room in the brownstone where she lived on Gold Street.

We all lived near each other but in our own apartments. So she took my hand and led me back into her room. It wasn't my first time, but it felt like it was. When we met Jake later at a pizza joint down the street for dinner, we made sure to come from separate directions. It was hard, but we never let on.

And then we had an even bigger problem.

Maybe it was the work we did for the police. Or maybe for the people who couldn't go to the police. But we got noticed. By the mob. They had all but destroyed my father, and now they wanted their due from us. So we paid. Protection money. Every week, a goon would come around, and we'd pay him. I would never have done it and neither would Jake, but they let us know that it was Ellen who they'd take it out on. I think they knew I was in love with her and sleeping with her. People like that always seem to horn in on your vulnerabilities.

Ellen knew about the payoffs, but she never found out why we went along with it so willingly. They started out small but quickly raised the price. They bled us dry, until we had hardly anything left to give. We were just about broke when the Colombians showed up.

"Don't worry about your friends down the block," the man with the thick black hair and the disarming smile told us. "We're buying out their interest. Just get our merchandise to shore safely."

They had a scheme that they had used in South America. They'd drop their shipment offshore. We decided on a spot just off Montauk, at the far end of Long Island. Sometime later, we'd go out and salvage the goods and bring them to shore. They couldn't do it themselves, because the feds knew who they were. We, on the other hand, were legit, and we knew how to run a salvage operation. So we did their dirty work, and now *they* protected us. When our local Mafia bagman turned up with his throat cut, I didn't ask any questions. The money was fantastic and no more payments to the mob. Just a little payback for my old man. As long as we got that merchandise to shore safely.

And we did. And *that* got us noticed too.

The merchandise, as it turned out, was high grade heroin. And there was a drug war with a terrorist front group stretching all the way to Afghanistan. They were Persian. And they knew we were Persian too. At least two-thirds of us.

When *they* paid a visit, the man who came spoke in Persian. He didn't know I understood. Jake and Ellen stood like stone tablets as he pressed them into service for Allah. It wasn't good. A drug war. But the Persians didn't want us to bring in just drugs. They also wanted weapons—guns and explosives— smuggled into the country. It was a religious war too. And we were in the middle of it.

Jake told the man, who was tall with light eyes and a neatly trimmed beard, that he would think about it. But we all seemed to realize that that meant no. A little drug smuggling to get the Mafia off our backs was one thing, helping terrorists kill innocent people was another.

This time, it wasn't Ellen that they threatened.

"You're friend over there," the man said smiling, still speaking in Persian. "His head would look nice on a stick out in your boatyard."

Jake opened his mouth to speak, but Ellen cut him off before he got the chance. "You filthy maggots! You destroyed Iran, and now you want to spread your poison here! Well get out!"

The man laughed at her then turned to Jake. "You aren't much of a man are you? In bed with infidels; you can't even control your women." He shook his head. "I'll bet this one is fucking your sister."

I put on my best poker face and made sure not to look at Ellen. Or Jake.

"I'll be back tomorrow," the man said, turning to leave. "Our first shipment is due in after sunset. Be ready to go by seven."

I had never seen Jake so rattled or so angry. We talked over our options. Should we go to the police? The FBI? Should we make a run for it?

I reminded them that the Colombians had a shipment that afternoon, and there'd be hell to pay if we failed to deliver. Then there was a noise outside the door. Jake, his blood now boiling, went to get it. He took a pistol out of the drawer, and Ellen and I looked at each other, wondering what he would do if it was the Persian man again, or what would happen if it was the Colombians. Or just the mailman. I thought about the Persian man's comment about her and me and wondered if it was just talk or if it was that obvious and if it tipped Jake off.

The gun dangled as he opened the door, but there was no one there. Just a package: a dead fish wrapped in newspaper. A Sicilian message. We'd be going where that fish came from very soon.

We were in over our heads, and we knew it. So we decided to make a run for it, get the hell out of town before it was too late. Ellen would go back to our apartments and pack for us, while Jake closed up the office and destroyed all our records. I would go into Manhattan and get our money and close out the bank account.

We'd meet downtown at the World Trade Center, take the train across to Newark, and get a bus to somewhere far away, somewhere where they'd never find us. Making our escape from Newark—the irony seemed to hang in the air between us.

Ellen and I left Jake in the office and went our separate ways, agreeing to meet later, in Midtown, for a quick rendezvous before heading to the Trade Center to meet up. We'd be careful, as always, not to show up at the same time.

Everything went smoothly. I got a check made out to cash for the balance in our account—a little over forty thousand dollars. I met Ellen outside the bank, just in front of the subway stop on Lexington Avenue. I gave her the check and kissed her, giving her butt one last squeeze, and she let out a smile.

"I'll see you down there at five, she said, before turning and disappearing down the subway station.

II

I'm thinking about it all, recalling the whole episode as I savor the taste of her on my lips and the feeling of her ass against my hand. In my dream, I fail to notice the footsteps behind me. Then I turn and see. Two men closing in on me fast. The Colombians? The Persians? The Mafia? I turn to look down Lexington, but there are two more men closing in and cutting off my escape to the south.

So I turn and run in the only direction available: west onto Lexington Avenue, into moving traffic. A cab skids to a stop as I weave through the moving cars. Two more of them narrowly miss me, but I make it across.

"Get him!" I hear one of the men yell. Looking back, I see him head for a car with the second man, while the other two chase me on foot. I head up Lex, against traffic, forcing them to come after me on foot. They're still trying to make it across when I round the corner of 64th, heading west, towards Central Park. I cross Park Avenue then Madison, finally hitting 5th. By now, they are only a block behind me.

I enter the park at 64th and pass Central Park Zoo before crossing the 65th Street transverse and gaining the shadows and darkness of the park's trees. Like when I was a kid playing cowboys and Indians, I run through the park dodging outcroppings of Manhattan schist as I flee my enemies. The sound of breaking branches and crushed leaves tells me that they are only a hundred or so yards behind me.

The thought of hiding under a pile of leaves flits through my mind, even though I know it's ridiculous. Still in a sprint, I pass Bethesda Fountain and the Boat House, staying in among the trees. My shirt is soaked with sweat, and my lungs are tightening, but the two of them are still on my tail.

Veering west, I stay in the woods alongside the reservoir. I'm not sure how close they are, but I keep heading north.

As I pass North Meadow, sweat rolls down into my eyes. I'm in good shape, but I'm not used to the run, and we've gone almost three miles. I don't hear anything behind me. Maybe I've shaken them. Maybe I'm home free.

I'm in the most densely forested part of the park now, approaching the northern edge. This tract, from 106th Street to 110th, I remember my father telling me, was not originally to be included in the park, but the steep cliffs and rocky outcroppings made it unsuitable for development, so, it was added to the design at the last minute. Maybe there's a place to hide.

Without warning, the noise behind me is back. Climbing a set of rough-hewn steps through the trees, my legs feel like sandbags are attached to them. I can see an old brick utility house that looks like a small fortress with the American flag flying high against the off-black sky. I make it to its base and am halfway up its stone wall before he catches up to me.

"You're done," he says, mustering enough energy to not sound out of breath.

Dropping off the wall, I turn and face him, expecting to die. Then I see the bad suit and a glint of gold, and I realize. The cops. A moment later, he flashes his FBI badge and cuffs me.

A minute after that, and the other one catches up. Then the car screams in from the northwest corner of the park, and before I know it, I'm in the back seat, still cuffed, on my way downtown.

I enter the Tombs, the lockup in Lower Manhattan, through the back end of Bayard Street. It *looks* like a basement prison, concrete-faced, with slit-eyed windows. Walking through the brown doors surrounded by cops and agents in suits, I feel like a guppy being swallowed by a whale.

It's yellow inside with long corridors that seem to lead nowhere. The linoleum floor tiles are the same as my high school cafeteria.

By the time I'm sitting in a metal chair in the interrogation room, the relief at not being killed has turned to dread. I'm going to jail. Probably for a long time. The room is hot. There's not even a ceiling fan. It smells like stale cigarettes and bad coffee. The only noise besides my own breathing is the hum of the twin fluorescent bulbs overhead. When I look up at them, I can see dark spots where flying insects, drawn to the light and heat, met their deaths and came to rest inside the white plastic case.

The door opens. It's a middle-aged man with the hard face of the FBI. He grimaces at me and sits down, facing me across the table with folded hands.

"I'd offer you some coffee, but the machine's broken," he says. Then he throws it out there. "We know about the Colombians."

I meet his stare but say nothing. *Does this mean that they don't know about the Persians?*

"What Colombians?" I ask, with the preposterous air of a guilty man pretending to be innocent.

"So that's the way it's going to be," he says, leaning back. "You know, drug trafficking is serious shit, Bill. We're talking life in prison."

My heart sinks.

"And I don't think you can do it. I don't think you'll last five minutes on the inside."

He's probably right, and I think to ask for my phone call, but I don't even know a lawyer. So I ask him straight out. "What do you want from me?" And I'm figuring he's going to press me to turn on the Colombians and give up everything I know, but he doesn't.

"We want your friend."

"Huh?" it takes me a second to realize. "You mean Jake?"

He nods. "That's right."

"Why?"

"We already know everything you know about the Colombians and a lot more." He pauses for a second, and I know they don't have enough evidence to get them, and they need to nail *somebody*. And I suddenly realize that they want a scapegoat. "But somebody's got to go down for this. To set an example, maybe get a little decent press for the good guys." And he looks straight at me. "And I don't give a shit whether its you or him." He sits back. "Whoever gives it up first walks. The other guy is going to *need* a walker by the time he gets out of prison." Another pause and another look. 'Think about it."

Then the door opens, and a blonde woman in a grey skirt suit calls him over. She's in her forties with a decent face and nice figure, but she looks even tougher than he does.

I'm alone in there for maybe twenty minutes, looking up at the two-way glass now and then, trying to look nonchalant but ready to pop out of my skin.

Then the door opens, and the blonde woman enters and sits across from me. She strokes her arm under her backside to keep her skirt straight as she sits, and I can hear the snug wool creak just barely perceptible against her nylon hose. Methodical, thorough, and patient.

She forces a smile at me, and I can't tell whether she's a kind woman pretending to be hard or a hard woman pretending to be kind.

Either way, I know she's being doing this for a while and she's good at it.

"We've got your friend," she tells me. "He didn't want to talk at first, but then we told him about you and his sister. That seemed to loosen him up a bit. After that, he told us everything."

"What do you mean?" I ask, showing more alarm than I want to.

"He told us about your deal with the Colombians, how they took the heat off from the mob." Then she paused and looked straight at me. "How it was all you, that he and his sister weren't really involved."

I sit looking at her and say nothing.

"You're going to jail for a long time."

She's just about the age my mother was when she died, and I wish I had had my mother there to tell me what to do.

"If you have a different version of things, I'm listening. Now would be the time to tell us, Bill."

I don't know if they're lying to me or not, but she, the other agent, and a third man take turns grilling me for the next three and a half hours. I don't tell them anything. The whole time I'm thinking about Jake and Ellen. And then, finally, when I've had enough, I look up and tell the woman, "I want my phone call now."

So two guards bring me into a room, and I give them Ellen's number to call.

"Hello?" I hear her sweet voice answer.

"Yasmin, it's Bill," I tell her, using her mother's name to let her know the call is being monitored.

"Are you all right?" she asks, keeping a lid on her obvious worry. She seems to get it.

"Yes, yes," I tell her. "But I'm in jail. So don't wait for me for dinner."

She seems to get that too. *Proceed with the plan. Use the forty grand. Get as far away from here as possible.*

I can hear her voice crack when she speaks. I know they're looking for her too, and, even if she didn't before, she does now. "I won't."

"I don't know if I'll see you again," I tell her.

"You can always see me anytime you want. Just recite my favorite poem—you remember the one—and I'll be there."

It's a sweet thing to say, even if a little off: After all, *She* was the one who used to recite that poem to *me*. But no matter. I savor the moment, then it's gone.

"Time's up."

"Au revoir," she says. It's something the Persians like to do—throw in a little French—but not something I recall her ever doing. But I savor that too.

When I hang up, the guards bring me back out, and the blonde woman tells me that they're stopping the interrogation for the night. "Here's my card in case there's something you want to tell me," she says, writing an additional phone number on the back. "That's my personal cell number."

I look at her name, Jennifer Wilkins, and I'm wondering why she's giving me the card now, thinking I'm going to see her in the morning when they start back up. Then she tells me that in the morning they'll be taking me to a federal prison in Lewisburg,

Pennsylvania. I don't know what happens after that, but I figure it only gets worse from here.

III

I open my eyes and stare at the ceiling as the buzzer goes off. Six a.m. wakeup. I don't like waking up in prison. Even the artificial light—the only kind you get down here in the bottom cell block—is simultaneously dull and harsh.

I wash at the sink. It's a simple white affair, with double spigots, like a laundry room basin. Rust seeps out from where the enamel is worn away, but there's a fresh bar of soap.

There's no cafeteria here, and breakfast is served on a plain metal tray, slipped through a slot in the bars. Bacon and eggs, coffee, and a piece of buttered toast. *Room service*, I think to myself, as I inspect my meal. *Not bad.* The coffee tastes like Drano, but the eggs are okay, even though I'm sure they're powdered. I eat the bacon last.

When they come to get me, the guard asks if I need anything. I tell him no, as I get up and leave the cell. I don't even look at him when I answer.

Up the stairs and down the hall, we move like rats in a maze, until we're finally out the back exit. I expect a police van—the paddy wagon—or at least a squad car, but we're to make the trip in a plain green Chevy sedan.

Three agents are waiting by the car. The one in the center is shorter that the other two and looks like he's been wearing the same suit for days.

"We ready?" asks the man on his left, medium-height, but broad-shouldered with a blond crew cut that makes him look like a Marine on steroids.

"Yeah, he's all yours," answers my escort, who I finally notice for the first time, his thin gray hair and bad breath screaming of Colt .45 Malt Liquor and a Swanson's TV dinner.

The third agent is nondescript, with green-lensed Ray Ban aviators that seem to hang over his concave cheeks which, as near as I can tell from their wrinkle-free surface, have barely ever registered emotion.

Ray Ban opens the driver's door and slips in, while Steroids gets in the other side. Shorty waits to open the back.

"Hold on," he says. "Got to cuff you."

He takes out a set of chrome cuffs and locks our wrists together before we slide in. There are no interior handles, and he has to grab the arm rest to pull the door shut. Within a few seconds, we are on our way.

We ride down Canal Street, across Manhattan Island, and through the Holland Tunnel into Jersey. We pass a cheap motor lodge, two gas stations, and a bar, before we're on the Turnpike. I look over at New York, directly across. The Statue of Liberty is in the foreground, with her back to me. She seems close enough to touch.

I watch the other cars going by. The Turnpike is crowded, and I think of a girl from my class in high school who was also from Jersey. I can't remember her name, but she was skinny with thick glasses and studied all the time. I saw her crying once, in the library, back in the stacks. I debated whether to ask her what was wrong and if I could help, and I finally overcame my reluctance and did just that. She didn't even look at me, telling me to go away in her shame. When I passed her in the hall two days later, we didn't even acknowledge each other.

Ellis Island pokes out from the top of the railing, looking as if it's resting on it. I know how close these islands are to the Jersey side, but it's still shocking to see them up close. Brooklyn now looms on the other side. A car blocks my view. It's also green, but the shade is lighter.

I wait for it to pass, but it doesn't. I glance over and see a man looking back at me. He's ugly, with a fleshy nose too small for his face. His window is open, and he lifts his arm like he's going to rest it on the sill. Then I see the gun.

I dive for the footwell, stopping only to grab Shorty's head and push it down with me. He resists for an instant, until the window pops and he realizes what's happening. There's another pop, and, looking up, I see Ray Ban's brains mixed with bits of safety glass over the top of the front seat. Steroids grabs for the wheel before catching one between the eyes and collapsing dead across the arm rest.

"Jesus Christ!" Shorty yells, blood spattered and dripping off his forehead.

Our car veers to the right, into the breakdown lane, scraping against the guard rail. This is an elevated section of the Turnpike, and if we don't get control of the wheel, we're going over the side, at least 30 feet to the ground below. The other car slams into us, driving us further into the guard rail.

I decide to make a move for the wheel, but Shorty stops me.

"I'll go," he says.

I get it. I'm the prisoner. *His* prisoner. But it doesn't matter, we're cuffed together anyway. He crawls headfirst through the crack between the front seats. I follow with my face practically in his ass. We stay low, peeking up just enough to see that we're at an exit—14A—Bayonne.

We crowd in amongst the two dead agents. The smell is familiar, fresh and salty. I take it in as we arc around the off ramp. Only one car can fit at a time, and, I can see in the rear view mirror, they have filed in behind us. The two men in the front seat are ordinary looking. One has on a Yankees t-shirt and the other has a small, oval head poking through a dark shirt that looks new but cheap, like his mother or girlfriend picked it out of the leftover bin at Wal-Mart.

Back down in the front foot well, there's a cell phone. The radio is next to it, bolted to the underside of the dashboard. Shorty pulls my arm up, as he finally puts both hands on the wheel, pushing Ray Ban's body to the side. I tumble over it, shoving him down over the other agent, the four of us crammed into the front seat of the Chevy like frat brothers on a road trip.

They're still behind us, but they're not shooting. They're probably waiting until they have us cornered or at least have a better angle. We fight to escape, careening down the exit and up another ramp onto a back highway, picking up speed. I see the huge oil refinery to our left, sitting, perched on the western edge of the harbor at Constable Hook.

We both eye the rearview mirror. The man in the passenger seat loads a fresh clip. Shorty looks down at the radio then at me. There's no time to call for help. My glance shifts to Ray Ban's gun hanging down off the seat.

"Touch that gun and I'll shoot you before they do," he says.

The back window explodes, the bullet whizzing between us and lodging in the dashboard. We gain a moment of respite when the road whips us around in a tight circle, through another off ramp, until we are at ground level, right up against the refinery. Another shot and the front tire blows out. Shorty struggles to control the car, but it goes up over the curb, flipping before hitting a cement barricade.

My head and limbs jumble with Ray Ban's, Steroid's, and Shorty's. Blood and glass hit my face, and my shoulder lands on the dome light, cracking it, just as the car comes to a stop, upside down, on a patch of grass, crushed against the concrete.

I'm okay, free to move, except my hand, which is still cuffed to Shorty's wrist. I look over at him as the men behind us skid to a stop. He's alive, but his face is grimacing in pain. The dash and steering wheel have him pinned to the seat. His chest looks crushed.

"Give me the keys," I say.

The doors to the car behind us click open.

He pauses a second before speaking, "In my pocket."

I reach in and, without thinking, uncuff his side first.

The doors behind us slam shut, three of them. Then footsteps. I glance around but don't see a gun.

"Tell my wife that I love her," he says.

I nod then push my way through the front windshield. It's shattered but still in one piece, flexible like a spider web. I scramble out under the hood, still clutching the key, with the cuff dangling off my wrist. Moving around the barricade, I run down Hook Road into the refinery, hidden from view by the wreck.

Two quick gunshots tell me that they've killed Shorty. They'll see the other two bodies and be after me in a moment. I look for a place to hide. There are several distillation towers and blocks of huge circular oil tanks. I head for the tank farm.

Slipping between the white cylinders, I know I'm probably only a minute or so ahead of them. Oil stains and rust mar the paint and give each one a unique look. The sand beneath my feet makes me think of an hourglass running out.

I pick the nearest one and climb the ladder, mounted on the side, to the top. Looking around, I spot a tank with an open top, empty, probably for maintenance. I climb back down and run through the white forest to the tank with the Rorschach splotch that looks like a Pennsylvania Dutch hex sign. Up the ladder and down the other side, I am now at the bottom of the open tank. It's enormous inside. There is some kind of detergent on the bottom, about an inch deep, but the smell of petroleum, sickly sweet, appealing at first, then nauseating, is overpowering.

Inside the tank is a rippling sound, like the sheet metal of an air conditioning duct—the wind mixing with the hum of the distillation towers, amplified inside the hollow shell, but otherwise, all is quiet. Maybe they've gone, I think to myself, but then I realize: They're waiting. Waiting for dark.

Night falls, and they come.

IV

One time when I was five years old, we were crossing the Turnpike Bridge, coming back from the city. I was lying on the back seat, looking up, and I saw the sunset through the front windshield, between my parents. I watched it for several minutes over Newark Bay as we passed that refinery on Constable Hook, the Twin Towers shimmering pastel shades through the rearview mirror from the other direction.

Over the rim of the oil tank, the sky changes color once again—orange, pink, blue, until, finally, only the lights from the distillation tower shine. The cleaning fluid at the bottom burns my waterlogged skin. The cuffs hang three rungs up on the inside ladder, my only weapon. I wait and listen. Another hour passes, then two. The men outside are waiting, waiting for me to make my move.

I debate my options: Sit and wait. But my skin is on fire, and my lungs ache from the fumes. Or I could make a break across the railroad tracks into the residential area of Bayonne. But it's open space, I'd be a sitting duck. Besides, I'd probably end up getting some innocent people killed. No more of that.

Then my mind drifts to the Atlas Yacht Club. I wonder if it's still there. If it is, it would be closer, and I'd have the cover of the refinery and those huge white tanks. I ponder the odds and decide to take the risk. This is, after all, a maritime town, and old sea hands tend to cling to these things. And chances are these men are not sailors. Most people aren't. Yeah, out on the open water, that's my best shot.

Slowly and quietly, I move for the ladder. Every sound is amplified inside the empty cavity of the tank. Then sounds come in from the outside. Voices. Words.

Tin sounds of a man climbing an adjacent tank, then more words. I still can't understand them, but I figure he's seeking a perch to look out over the landscape for where I might be hiding. When the footsteps come back down, I know one of them will be coming here, into the empty tank.

More footsteps, this time on the outside of *my* tank. I slide in behind the inside ladder, grabbing the cuffs. When he comes over the top, I can see his shadow, even the stubble of his beard. His movements are confident, like a hunter, with no sign of fear. He steps down the ladder, looking down around the inside. I just escape his field of view.

He descends, rung-by-rung, until his feet are only a few inches from my face. I think to punch him in the crotch, but I have to keep him quiet. He continues down, still unaware of my presence, gun clanging off steel, until he is nearly face-to-face with me.

When his foot hits water, I jump out, wrapping the cuffs around his neck from behind. He flips me over the top of his head, landing me flat on my back in a splash, but the pistol drops, disappearing into the dark fluid. Adrenaline coursing through my veins, I spring to my feet, turning to face him.

For the first time, I get a good look at his face. It's the man with the ugly nose. On his left cheek, the one that was facing away from me in the car, is a long, deep chasm.

He pulls out a switchblade and snaps it open. The moonlight glows off the metal.

"I'm going to cut your eyes out," he says in a thick Persian accent, and I suddenly know who sent these men.

I look down to the spot where the gun dropped in the water. His eyes follow by reflex, and I slap the cuff on the hand holding the knife. Jerking him down, I pull his arm to the ladder and lock the other cuff around the bottom rung.

Planting my heel into his wrist, I crush it against the metal, forcing the knife from his hand. He grabs my ankle as I climb the ladder, but I kick him in the face and pull free, scrambling up to the top as he yells to warn the other two.

When I reach the lip, I look around. The coast is still clear. The others must be fanned out, but it won't take them long to get here. I drop down the side back onto the sand of the Hook. He continues to shout. They call back, and I get a sense of how close they are.

I spot a pipe with a large valve going into the bottom of the tank. Grabbing with both hands, I try to turn it, but it won't budge. I kick it as hard as I can, several times, finally moving it maybe an inch. Laying my hands back on it, I turn it all the way. Oil flows into the tank. Skin, flesh, and bone frantically bang metal inside, the hollow sound gradually subsumed by thick, viscous crude. *One down, two to go.*

Footsteps crunching in the sand come at me from two directions, both off the harbor, oblique to the Kill and where the Atlas Club is—or used to be. I glance back, spying the upper bay, shiny, placid, at high tide, her waters ready to recede.

My feet move south, almost in a dance, over puddles of oil mixed with sand, to the Kill and, I hope, the

Atlas Club. The knock of grains against metal tells me that they have picked up my trail and aren't far behind. Voices, now clearly Persian, and the sounds of guns cocking catch up to me. Then that sound, of a bullet expelled through a muzzle, whizzing past my head an instant later. All I see ahead of me is darkness. Another shot, closer this time.

Running by a set of processing pipes and a distillation tower, I find myself surrounded by gravestones, crumbling, weather-beaten, with Dutch inscriptions—a family cemetery, an island, preserved in the sea of oil. I think to hide behind its monuments but realize that it's futile. There is one last tanker and something beyond, white and silver, rectangular. Nick's Luncheonette. I dart between it and the last tank.

Inside are the red stools and white counter with bags of chips and rows of cups that I remember. The diner blocks their shots, as I leave it behind me. Now I see the Kill straight ahead, its waters just starting to move, whitecaps forming, the wind blowing in, picking up, against the growing tide. But no boat club. Only more swishing sand under thick-soled shoes, closing in.

Then, focusing out of the background, there she is, like a mirage, on that inlet of the Kill. I look behind

me and see them, maybe a city block or two away.
They don't shoot—they think they have me cornered.
I lead them out onto a wooden pier, gray, weather-
beaten. There are at least a dozen boats—sailing
boats, row boats, even a few yachts—most in some
state of disrepair but seaworthy. It looks almost
quaint, with Staten Island a few hundred yards in the
background.

I pick a small sailboat. It'll be hard to handle in the
wind, with the tide moving in the opposite direction,
but it should be fast. Untying the ropes, I step on
board and hoist the mainsail then the jib. A shot tears
through the empty space bulging between them as the
wind carries me away from the pier.

As I buck the waves moving west along the Kill
Van Kull, they pursue me. One of them unties another
sailboat, while the other shoots two more rounds in
my direction. But I'm too far away now, lying flat on
the deck, and he misses.

The tide has picked up, the water now flowing fast
out to sea. I buck the waves, riding downwind straight
into them, maneuvering my sail for maximum speed
and stability. The wind surrounds me and fills my
lungs. They've stopped shooting, now out in the middle of the Kill, further and further behind me. They've

gotten their sail up, but their boat is moving around in a circle. They're in trouble on this moonlit night, in a stiff cross breeze, with whitecap currents.

The boat is sideways to the current, and the sail catches the full brunt of the wind. In a turn that makes me grin from ear-to-ear, I watch their boat capsize. I slow down to see the two men and their vessel separated and sucked out to sea by the current. Even an Olympic swimmer would have trouble surviving.

When I lose sight of them, I feel a burst of pride then release my sail back into the wind, clearing Staten Island and entering Newark Bay. Continuing along, I approach the huge containers on the opposite shore. I guide her in, my hand still sure, breaking down the sail and slowing to a crawl as I approach the edge of the marine terminal—land, Newark. Slipping her in between two huge container ships, she bumps the steel bulkhead gently. Still at three quarters tide, I climb up onto the dock, holding the rope, ready to moor the sailboat to the thick steel post.

Staring down at her, dwarfed in the enormous berth, I throw the rope down on her deck and let the tide carry her out to sea.

V

I walk past containers, neatly stacked, like the shoeboxes in my mother's closet. Past that are rows and rows of new cars, thousands of them, ready to be loaded and taken to dealers in New York, New Jersey, Connecticut, Pennsylvania, and beyond. Fork lifts and freight elevators stand at the ready to get the job done.

I continue along the perimeter, still wet from the inside of the tank. It's a cool night, but I know my clothes will dry, and I know I'm alive. That puts me one up on the others, including the FBI. Shorty's voice creeps into my head, asking me to tell his wife that he loves her. Then hunger comes to the fore, and my mouth waters for Taylor Ham, soft white bread, and hot broken cookies.

At the end of the marine terminal, I jump a high chain-link fence and am practically on the New Jersey Turnpike. There are at least a dozen lanes and a frontage road. The bright lights of the toll plaza drive me north. As I look over my shoulder, there are also rail lines and Newark Airport buttressed firmly against the highway on the other side.

The road splits and turns, winding into a maze of on-ramps and off-ramps. Moving under and through,

I am finally across, walking along the northern edge of the airport. Steering clear of the cameras, I run into another maze of ramps and another toll plaza. At this juncture, there are at least thirty lanes. It's probably past ten at night, but there are still plenty of cars and trucks.

Like a trapped animal, I look for an exit. Across the highway, past the toll plaza, is another chain-link fence. Guard towers poke out from the coils of razor wire on top. A plain sign, in black and white announces: Northern State Prison. I swallow a hit of panic, glancing left, along the perimeter of the airport: another cluster of ramps. I decide to backtrack, heading east, back towards the water.

Back on the other side, near the water, I make my way north along the Turnpike, eventually crossing under it past the Newark Bay Bridge, the airport, and the prison. This part of Newark, the waterfront, is an industrial wasteland. I take it in, walking under Route 1—the Pulaski Skyway leading into Manhattan—then Route 9.

The landscape changes abruptly, residential houses replacing rail yards and smelting plants. A smell, distant, familiar, emerges. It's sweet and bready, and, for an instant, I mistake it for that cookie factory on Frelinghuysen Avenue. Looking around, I spot a smokestack and a neon sign in the distance, past the airport: an eagle flying, fading into a golden 'A' then back again, and I realize: The Budweiser factory.

I could actually use a cold one. And that Taylor Ham sandwich. But my pockets are empty. No cell phone, no credit cards, and not a dime. My clothes are starting to dry, and the wind is much less stiff than out on the open water, a mild breeze, pleasant even.

I continue wandering north, toward Penn Station in Newark, a good place to sleep. It's odd how the streets here echo the names of those across the river in Manhattan: Vesey, Pearl, Houston, Warren, and Delancy. Lafayette, Mott, and Maiden Lane. There's even a Wall Street.

Stepping over that endless array of freight tracks, the neighborhood turns, the houses bigger but older and more decrepit. And then I smell it: that mix of the Passaic River and Portuguese sweet bread. And then I see the sign: *Welcome to Ironbound, the Heart of Newark.* The same words appear underneath in Portuguese, next to a set of crossed flags, American and Portuguese, painted against the white background.

There still there—signs in Portuguese and a few in Spanish or Italian. The seafood restaurants keep my stomach grumbling for something to eat. It's past midnight, and they're all closed anyway. I can smell the garbage piled in the alleys, shellfish ripening in the temperate night air; olive oil and clam broth turning sour.

The eateries give way to an old factory, then another, which occupy the better part of two blocks. I follow my nose to the river, knowing that it will lead me to the train station, but run smack into the park—River Bank Park, where I played as a child with Jake and Ellen—still sitting there on the shore of the Passaic, where it bends around in a broad curve before looping over again to meet the Hackensack River at the top of Newark Bay. Some of the locals still call the neighborhood Down Neck, referring to the double-back loop of the river. The Dutch farmers called this whole area *Achter Kull*—behind the neck—but they were referring to the neck of land that holds Constable Hook.

Those Dutch farmers had a lot of necks. They're still here, ghosts on the land, names, cemeteries, words, and phrases. So are the Indians, the Weequaheks and the Hackensacks. I think of them as I lie under the stars, beside an oak tree, in the park, just up the bank from the river and its bend. My mother seeps into my mind. Then my father and his tugboat. Shorty and the other agents. The men in the oil refinery. Jake and Ellen. My eyes close, and I sleep.

The sun wakes me maybe five hours later, but I'm rested. I never needed much sleep, even when I was a kid. I'm so hungry I eye the acorns on the ground, fallen from the broad oak branches, like manna from heaven. Watching a squirrel clutching one of the nuts, chipping at the hard skin, I think better of it.

Exiting the park, I realize I need more than just food. I need new clothes, a place to sleep, a plan. I need *money*. Of course, they'll be looking for me, the police, the FBI. I feel the stubble on my face. A shower and a shave, that's what I need.

Or maybe not.

A beard and hair dye. Yeah, I need hair dye, first, before anything. Then I'll worry about the rest. It's still early, maybe 7 a.m., but there should be a drugstore open. On Market Street, past the intersection with Raymond Boulevard, near the corner of Union, I find what I'm looking for: A CVS. It's next to a Burger King, but I ignore my hunger pangs and enter the store.

The air conditioning is on full blast, and it's freezing cold inside. Walking the aisles, I find the hair dye, across from the candy. They know their clientele: fat, middle-aged women who want to look young and sexy again but can't resist a sugary treat. Suddenly, neither can I.

I palm a King Size Snickers Bar and gobble it down before anyone can see, stuffing the empty wrapper behind a box of gum. I turn back and look at the hair dye on the other side. Moving around, I catch a whiff of myself in the enclosed space. The stink is fierce.

The blue vest of an employee cuts through the aisles, heading my way. He looks down rather than make eye contact, and I know: He thinks I'm a bum. He's coming to roust me out of the store. Quickly, I take in the array of coloring: blond, red, black. *Black.* I grab a small Jet Black and stuff it in my sock then turn and grab four candy bars – two Tootsie Rolls, another Snickers, and a Reese's four pack, and stuff them in my pockets.

I rip open a Goldenberg's Peanut Chew, now in plain sight of him, and wolf it down. He pulls the half-empty package out of my hand.

"This isn't a restaurant," he says, glaring at me.

It doesn't really make any sense: You still have to *pay* in a restaurant, but I don't correct him. He's a young kid, probably in high school, probably working to make a few dollars, maybe for college or a used car, or maybe just to spend on a girl. He's probably a decent kid. I won't give him a hard time, even though I'm desperate.

"Okay, okay, I'm going," I say, taking a step in the direction of the door.

He stops me with his hand, even though his expression tells me that it repulses him to touch me.

"Empty your pockets."

I knew he'd see the candy. My hope was that it would distract him from the hair dye in my sock, the thing I really need.

I take out three of the bars and put them on the shelf.

"All of it," he says, keeping his eyes on my pockets.

I pull out the last one, the Reese's, and put it next to the others. The box of dye is digging into my ankle. He looks back, over his shoulder at an older man, in the same blue vest, writing a note, then leans his head in to me. I wait for him to say, *the hair dye too*, but he doesn't.

"Look, there's a shelter on McWhorter Street, down from the station," he whispers. "Real nice lady there runs it. A friend of my mother's. They'll give you something to eat."

He looks back again. "Don't let my boss know I told you, he hates bums." A flush of embarrassment crosses his face. "I mean vagrants." Then confusion. "I don't know what you like to be called."

For the first time, I look at his name tag: Francisco.

"Thank you," I say, looking into his small, dark eyes.

I turn towards the door and exit.

VI

My clothes are cotton, and I figure I can wash them out in the sink in the bathroom at the train station, maybe clean myself up too before I dump that black dye in my hair.

The CVS is at the intersection of Market Street and Raymond Boulevard, just up from its intersection with Commercial Street. After that sits Penn Station. I have butterflies in my stomach as I approach. It'll be crowded. People. Commuters. Lots of them. Cops. When I pass that last intersection, I notice a statue, surrounded by pigeons in a tiny park: Santa Francisca

Javiera Cabrini—Mother Cabrini—patron saint of immigrants and hospital administrators.

Her tomb is across the river, in Washington Heights, Manhattan, at the Mother Cabrini School for Girls on Fort Washington Avenue, around the corner from where I lived with my dad when we first moved to New York.

There's a cop right on the corner, at the front of the station. He's looking the other way, but I walk a block up to another entrance anyway. It's crowded but less than I was expecting. Like the other things here, it's a miniature of the one in New York—still big, but definitely smaller, less crowded, and cleaner than its sibling across the river.

The stick-figure silk-screened signs, white on blue, of a man and woman, call me across the main room to the bathroom in the corner.

I shuffle across, holding my breath, like a deranged homeless person, hoping that's all anyone will see, even as they look away. There's another cop, hands behind his back, on patrol. His nightstick, loose in his grip, peeks out from his beat blues. I fight the urge to turn, run, and try to hide, continuing my shuffle. He doesn't seem to notice me. Just another homeless person in Penn Station, Newark, New Jersey.

In my act, I almost walk into the wrong bathroom. An older woman looks horrified, and I realize my error. When I'm finally inside the men's room, I exhale. Stripping down to my boxers, I wash my pants and shirt with warm water and hand soap in the sink, letting them soak while washing myself in the basin next to it. The directions on the box are simple enough, and I work the dye into my hair like shampoo saving a pinch for the stubble on my face. Hesitating at first, I finally take my underwear off and wash it out while I wait for my hair to set.

Meanwhile, men come in and out, about half giving a cursory stare. The other half ignore me completely. Civilians aren't any more interested in a bum than the cops are. Most of them are in suits, commuters to Manhattan no doubt. I remember the train station from when I was a kid. We used to play here too. It looks the same only smaller.

After what feels like about twenty minutes, I wash my hair out, combing it back with my fingers. *Not bad*, I think, looking at myself in the mirror. Someone might even mistake me for Persian. In the other sink, my clothes look dull and grungy. On a whim, I add some of the dye, letting it stew for about five minutes. It turns my clothes gray, and when I wring them out and press them dry on the floor with what seems like an entire ream of paper towels, they don't look bad, stylish even, and they don't smell anymore.

They're still damp when I put them on, but I look okay. More important, I look different. The beard's not there yet, but I'll definitely be harder to recognize. I pass my first test when the cop walks into the bathroom, right past me, and unzips his fly at the urinal.

Crossing back through the station, with confidence this time, a woman even smiles at me. I hang out in the park, drying off under the sun, behind Mother Cabrini.

It's midday when I head out, down Union, over Ferry Street, to McWhorter. Seven or eight blocks later, I spot a white neon cross sticking out from a brown wooden church. I place the style even before I read that they're Baptists. The brick building next to it must be the homeless shelter. I walk up the steps, through tall wooden doors.

"Excuse me," I say to a man in jeans and a button-down shirt, out-of style, but clean. "Is this the shelter?"

I suddenly hope that I haven't done *too* good a job cleaning myself up. But he never looks at my clothes.

"No, this is the seminary," he tells me. "The kitchen, the shelter, they're in back, around the corner," he says, pointing.

The Seminary. Maybe I'll end up being a priest, I think to myself in a moment of insanity. Then I think of Ellen and how I'll never see her again, and a wave of sadness hits me. I recite the poem by Rumi in my head, and it helps. But I suddenly feel a wave of weakness as my blood sugar plummets after that Snickers Bar.

The smell tells me when I enter the right building. It's almost as bad as the Passaic River. Or the inside of that tank. There's nobody to greet me this time, and I wander down a corridor until the smell of b.o. gives way to soup, rice, and beans. I follow it to the kitchen, but the room seems empty, until I see a man standing in the doorway to an outside alley.

He's smoking a cigarette when I step up to him. Noticing me, he throws it down, half-smoked, crushes it under the toe of his shoe, and exhales in a forced rush of white smoke. *I'm not your boss*, I want to tell him, feeling slightly bad for depriving him of half his butt.

Feelings of shame and awkwardness leave me tongue-tied for an instant, but I fight them off. "Is this where I can get something to eat?" I ask.

He nods, smoke still trickling out of his mouth and nostrils. "Yeah, talk to her," he tells me, the nod morphing into a tilt of the head, forward, over my shoulder.

I turn around and see a white leg moving under a maroon skirt, disappearing around a door jamb.

"Thanks," I say, turning to pursue.

I catch up to her further down an adjacent hall, as she enters her office.

"Hi," I call from behind.

She's startled. Then turning and seeing me, she shows relief.

"Sorry, I didn't mean to scare you," I say, apologetically.

"That's okay," she says. "What can I do for you?"

She's middle-aged, mid-50s probably, petite but pretty, even though she has a haggard look.

"I just need a place to sleep and something to eat," I explain, having trouble getting the words out.

She nods. Her hair is black, dyed no doubt, and I wonder what brand. She's only about 5'1, dark eyes and a pale face. The heels give her an extra few inches, but she still only comes up to my chest.

"How long have you been out on the street?" she asks, matter-of-fact.

"Only a short time," I say, feeling ever-more embarrassed.

She nods again, expressionless. There's a sadness about her, a woman worn down by life. But something noble too, even classy. Standing straight and proud, she has perfect posture. She's kind, and I like her immediately.

"We could use somebody to clean up around here, but I can't pay you," she offers.

"I'd be delighted," I tell her, without hesitating, unable to say no to the kindly mother-figure. I regret it as soon as the words are out, but then I finally see her smile, and it seems worth it. "Where are my manners," I say. "I'm Jake," I tell her, not wanting to use my real name.

Then, looking at the name on her desk, just behind her, I add, "And you must be Rachel Czyzyck," I say, pronouncing the Polish tongue-twister—CHIS-ick—perfectly.

Her eyebrows raise, her smile widens, and she laughs. "*VERY* good! I still have trouble with it sometimes, and I've had 30 years to practice."

"You don't look a day over 29," I tell her, grinning.

She smiles a little then rolls her eyes and shakes her head. "It was my husband's name. He's dead. Heart attack at 39," she sighs. "I'll show you the janitor's closet. By the way, dinner's at five."

I'm enjoying talking to Rachel Czyzyck, and I can tell that she's enjoying it too. She's lonely, and it makes me sad. She's the kind of woman who loved her husband too much to ever be with another man, and that makes me sad for her. And maybe for myself.

"This neighborhood used to be all Polish and Italian," she tells me. *I know that,* I want to say, but I keep my mouth shut. "My husband was from here, so this is where we ended up, but I'm from Manhattan originally," she tells me. "You've been to college, haven't you?" she asks, stopping at another wooden door, sliding a key in, and opening it.

"Yes," I answer.

She looks over at me, her body canted slightly as she opens the door, holding it in place with her foot, and pulls the key out. "Me too. Vassar, class of '85."

VII

I clean the downstairs bathroom and sweep the halls. I'm actually grateful to have something to do, something to keep me busy, something useful. By the time dinner rolls around, I am so hungry I'm ready to pass out. It's turkey pot pie, and it's actually okay. I eat till my stomach hurts.

I try to strike up a conversation with a couple of different people, but most of them are either mentally ill or just want to keep to themselves. One man mentions something about the internet. My ears perk up. "Yeah, they'll let you on for fifteen minutes at a time if the connection's up."

I have to wait almost an hour, but I get on. Two bodies turned up in the Lower Bay, off Coney Island. No mention of the boats, but maybe they'll think I died too. Maybe not. I need to think, figure out my next move. I hope that Jake and Ellen are far away, safe and sound. I may never have the privilege of knowing. There's nothing I can do about it now anyway, so I'll lay low, stay here for a few days, and catch my breath.

"Hey asshole, your time's up," a voice yells at me from behind.

I log out without answering and walk through a set of double doors to a big room with rows of beds. I stare out the window at downtown Newark, lit-up, pretty, with its gold-domed, Beaux-Arts city hall at the center, and I imagine the city in its heyday, the '30s and '40s, when my grandparents were kids, when Dutch Schultz held court here, before he was gunned down at the Palace in 1935, a story I heard many times from my father.

Parts of the city seem to be making a comeback, but swaths are still laid waste from the riots of the 1960s. The view out the other side of the building, of New York—Manhattan—is blocked.

I take off my clothes and get into my cot. The sheets are tight and rough, but I'm grateful for the clean smell of bleach. Still, the bed is even worse than the one at the Tombs.

Over the next few days, I slip into a routine at the shelter. Cleaning, helping in the kitchen, even helping Rachel in her office. She lets me pick out new clothes in the Mission Thrift Store. I actually find a decent shirt and pants, while a homeless woman with leathery, sunburned skin and no teeth turns down a free pair of sneakers because she doesn't like the way they look. "Women," the man behind the cash register says to me, shaking his head. I nod politely.

Rachel even trusts me with the collection box, despite the fact that she hardly knows me. I count it all out for her, putting the paper money in an envelope and rolling up all the change. After that, I help her move boxes of old files in her office, and, without warning, it's night.

She offers me a drink. I'm surprised to find that she likes scotch, single malt, the good stuff. She tells me about her husband and how he made her laugh, and I tell her about Ellen. She doesn't say anything, doesn't even seem surprised that there's a woman out there who loves me, who I love. She just nods and throws back another drink. So, there we are, the two of us, in the back office of the McWhorter Street Homeless shelter, sitting, talking, getting drunk.

I catch a glimpse of her knees. She always wears skirts, mid-length, and I haven't seen them before. I have to admit, I'm enjoying the view. Half of me wants to kiss her; the other half knows it's wrong, that it would be a disaster, that she doesn't want it, and that I'd feel awful afterwards.

She sees my eyes, my expression. Maybe it's the alcohol, but I can't hide it. She's one step ahead of me, cutting me off at the pass.

"You'd never believe it, but every once in a while, a guy'll drag himself in here and actually hit on me," she says, not moving an inch.

I pull my eyes back to her face, smile at her, and take another gulp. "I'm sorry, Rachel, I didn't mean to stare."

Now she knows her hunch was right. She looks me straight in the eye. "You're a very handsome man," she tells me. "But you know, I'm too old for you, and you're homeless." She takes another drink. "I didn't mean to lead you on," she adds. "I just get very lonely sometimes. You know, for someone to talk to."

She has delicate features, a china doll nose. Her cheeks sag a little, and there are creases around her mouth. She looks her age, but in a good way. She can see I'm not threatening. I never was with women.

"Go out and find your girl," she tells me. "Ellen," she says, adding her name, almost savoring it. "You don't get many chances in this world. You'll regret if it you don't."

"Thanks, Rachel," I say, getting up to leave.

She nods, sucking the dregs of her glass as I step out of her office.

I wake up hung-over the next morning. I'm feeling better by lunchtime, but I still don't know what to do with myself. I've been avoiding Rachel all day. I know it's time for me to move on, I just don't know where to go or what to do.

So I get on the computer and read *The New York Times* to kill a few minutes when I see his picture. I can hardly believe it, there on the front page of the arts section, the man who came to see us at our office in the boatyard on that last day—the Persian man, the terrorist! I see his name: Armin Moridi. And I read the headline: *A Philanthropist Takes Aim at Extremists—On Both Sides.*

I read the article. This man, Moridi, is a billionaire, made his fortune in oil futures. His background is murky, but he was born in Iran to one of the tribal groups in the hilly interior of the country, thought to be descended from the Iran's Aryan forbears. He fled to England as a young man, was educated at Oxford and King's College London, and went into business trading heating oil at first then crude futures, eventually relocating to New York.

Now, he was opening an interfaith center for "dialogue and understanding" near a mosque in Midtown Manhattan.

I look at his features: light hair and eyes, self-satisfied Mona Lisa smile, slightly crooked nose. It's definitely him, the man who came to see us, who threatened us, who wanted us to bring drugs and weapons into the country. The man who wanted my head on a stick! But how could it be? Is he working for the Feds? No, they'd never leave him out there like that. Besides, they'd never have sent him in to visit us like that either. And the fact that the Persians came to kill me and offed three of their agents . . . no, this man really is a terrorist, hiding in plain sight.

But why did he come to see us in person? Maybe this operation was too important to trust to a lackey. So he paid us a visit in person. And who were we to say no? If we went to the authorities, he'd tell them that we were crazy and then have us killed—Hell, we didn't even say anything, and he tried his best to kill me anyway. Who were they going to believe? A straight-and-narrow billionaire or three waterfront rats working for a Colombian drug lord?

And suddenly I think about Jake and Ellen. They're in terrible danger—worse, even, than I realized. I'd do anything to see her just one more time. Hold her, hug her. Warn her and protect her.

I think about what she said on the phone that last time I spoke to her: *You can always see me anytime you want. Just recite my favorite poem—you remember the one—and I'll be there.* Then finishing with *au revoir*—until I see you again.

Her favorite poem, *The Guest House,* by Rumi. She used to recite it to me from memory when I would stay over with her and Jake, when we were kids, after my mother died and my father started to drink. She wanted me to know that I should never feel bad about staying at their place, because I was always welcome. *Be grateful for whoever comes,* she would say quoting the poem. "And you aren't just anyone!" She would add. And I would feel better.

Yes, *The Guesthouse. My* guesthouse, as she would say when we were kids, and I suddenly realize where they are.

VIII

It's not far away. So I venture out of the shelter, down McWhorter then over to Ferry Street and down Prospect. I haven't seen it since I was a kid, but I recognize the house immediately.

As I approach, my heart beats faster. What if I'm wrong, and they're not there? I walk up the steps and knock. Then I see the bell and ring it.

I'm about to ring it again, when the door opens. A middle-aged man answers. He looks Iranian, but that doesn't mean my friends are there or that he even knows them.

He looks at me, looks around, and takes me by the arm. "Come in."

So I step in and he closes the door behind me. "Wait here," he tells me. Then, as an afterthought, he stops in his tracks and looks back at me. "You're Bill, right?"

I smile. "Yes."

And he smiles back. He's in his mid-fifties with dark skin, a slight belly, and a salt-and-pepper moustache. He gestures to the living room, "Please have a seat. I'll be right back."

So I sit while he disappears upstairs. Then I stand, a bundle of nerves. Then I see Ellen coming down the stairs, Jake behind her. She sees me, bolts down, and gives me a hug. Jake follows and squeezes my shoulder. I turn and hug him too.

He looks at me and grins, "Trying to look Persian?"

"Nah, just a bad dye job," I say, smiling back.

There they are, safe and sound. He doesn't know, I think. The cops lied. They never arrested him at all.

"When you didn't show up on Friday, we came straight here," Jake tells me, and my suspicion is confirmed. "Then, when you called—"

"I figured you'd get the clue," Ellen says, bursting a grin, and I nod back.

"Here, let's go in the kitchen," the man with the salt-and-pepper moustache says. "By the way, I'm Farhad."

A moment later we're in the kitchen, and I meet his wife, Fariba.

I learn that they're not really cousins but just close family friends from the old country, where they were declared enemies of the state, and they want to help as much as they can.

We talk for over an hour. "You have to go to the police," Farhad says, and my heart drops. I know we're in way too deep with the Colombians to stay out of jail; and the Colombians, the Mafia, and the Persian terrorists all have tentacles deep in the prison system. If we end up there, we're all dead.

Jake tells him as much, and we all seem to understand it. I can tell that Fariba has a deep mistrust of the authorities anyway.

Then we talk about fleeing. It has its problems but seems like the best option. But I don't like it. "Spending the rest of your life looking over your shoulder is no way to live," I tell them. "Only free when you're dead."

"Yeah, great. Only free when you're dead," Jake repeats, and it gives me an idea.

"I need a burner phone," I announce. "You know, pay-as-you-go," and I reach into my pocket and pull out the card that the blonde lady from the FBI gave me. The card is a mess but still legible: Agent Jennifer Wilkins. And there it is, her private cell phone number on the back.

I tell them what I'm thinking, and Farhad goes out to buy a phone.

When he comes back, we have dinner and talk like it's just an ordinary night with some old friends sharing a meal and good conversation. I've cleaned up and borrowed some clothes from their son who is away at college, and sitting there sipping Persian tea in the old house on Prospect, I almost forget what I have to do.

I wait until almost midnight and then call Agent Wilkins on her cell phone, when, I'm guessing, she's not at the FBI office. I don't think they can track it—a call from burner phone to her private cell number when she's away at the office—but I have to take the chance.

"Hello," I hear her answer, not groggy at all. I recognize her voice immediately.

"Hello, Agent Wilkins," I answer back.

"Where are you, Bill?" she asks, recognizing my
voice right away too. I'm surprised, but maybe I
shouldn't be. She's smart, and she's trained, and they
must know that I'm alive. I'm sure they've been looking for me.

"I know who killed your agents," I tell her. "But I
need something from you first."

"I'm listening."

So I tell her about the man who came to see us an
hour before they arrested me. That he wanted us
to bring drugs and weapons into the country and that
he was the head of an Iranian terrorist cell. I tell her
that we refused point blank and that he wasn't about
to take no for an answer. I tell her we're trapped. That
the only way out for us is "to die."

She gets that right away too. "You want us to fake
your deaths?"

"Yes," I tell her.

"I can't do that," she tells me.

"I know it's asking a lot. I know we've broken the
law. And I don't really have anything besides that
name. You don't need my testimony—the three men

who killed your agents are already dead—and there's nothing that I can give you, besides circumstantial evidence, to tie him to them anyway." Then I pause. "But you have no clue who's heading this terrorist cell, and believe me, this name is worth it."

"Okay," she says. "Give me the name, and I'll check it out. If it's as hot as you say, we'll talk."

"How are you going to contact me?" I ask.

"I already know where you are," she tells me, and my blood runs cold. "Sit tight. You'll hear from me in the next twenty-four hours. The safest thing for you to do is stay where you are." There's a pregnant pause. "So, what's the name?"

So I tell her, hoping she's more kind than tough and figuring they'll probably come and arrest us if I don't. "Armin Moridi."

Her answer surprises me. "You're out of your mind. He's actually been helping us."

Her shock is real—I'm sure she didn't mean to tell me that last part, but I'm ready. "The perfect cover. He's your man."

So we wait, and our minds wander. What if I'm mistaken? What if they can't find anything and don't believe me? What if they come and arrest us all? What if the Mob or the Colombians, or, God help us, the Persians come and find us here first?

Then, almost exactly twenty-four hours later, the burner phone rings.

Everything I told her checks out. It's hard to believe, but there it is. Moridi is probably a spy sent by the Revolutionary Guard, his cover and financing all ultimately supplied by Iran, channeled through various western banks and institutions. Probably a setup years in the making. It's going to take a massive operation to bring him down, but my part—our part—is done.

The request went all the way to Washington, but there's going to be a press release saying that they found us and that we were killed when they tried to take us alive. After that, they're sending us into witness relocation—reborn with new identities. She tells me that it would be safer to split us up, but they usually keep families together, and it is up to us.

I tell her to keep Jake and Ellen together and to send me somewhere else. "You know you'll never see them again," she says. "I know," I tell her, and I hang up.

Epilogue

GLEN HARBOR WISCONSIN, SIX MONTHS LATER

I am now Adam Daniels, teaching marine engineering at a small college on the western shore of Lake Michigan. It's winter, and I trudge across the quad, taking a shortcut through the snow. I'm renting a house near campus, and when I get there, I close the door and take my coat and boots off, and I don't notice. There are people sitting at my kitchen table.

My heart skips a beat, but then I see: Ellen and Jake.

"How—"

"Agent Jane," Jake says. "*You* may have agreed to cooperate, but *we* refused unless the FBI relocated us where they sent you."

I look at Ellen, and she looks down. Then I look right at Jake, and we lock eyes.

"I know," he tells me.

"For how long?"

"That you were in love with my sister?" He gives a wry look then glances over at her and back at me. He smiles. "Probably longer than you."

"I was afraid. You're so protective."

He puts his hand on my shoulder. "Have a little faith my friend. After what we've all been through together, I don't think there's anyone else I *would* trust with my sister."

I laugh. "Yeah, I guess so."

Later, over dinner, we talk about starting another salvage company.

"There's an old boat for sale down at the harbor," I tell them. "It'd be perfect to refit for salvage, and it's in good condition. The Great Lakes are fresh water, not as corrosive. And there are lots of wrecks."

Jake nods. "Yeah, this would a good place to start a salvage business."

I hold Ellen's hand under the table. "It's a cold winter, though," I tell them. "Much colder than back east."

Ellen nods. "Yeah, but the water's a lot cleaner." And we all laugh.

To see our other great titles,
visit us at:

BLACKBIRD BOOKS
www.bbirdbooks.com